This book belongs to

HANNAH LOUISE BOLDEN

CRISTMAS 2000

FROM NANNA ∨ GRAMPS-xxx

CONTENTS

NODDY

Pedigree

Published by Pedigree Books Limited
The Old Rectory, Matford Lane, Exeter EX2 4PS
Published in 2000
Copyright and trademarks are the property of Enid Blyton Limited (All rights reserved)

£6.99

WELCOME TO TOYLAND

HELLO, EVERYONE!

My name is Noddy and I live here, in Toy Town. Do you know where Toy Town is? It's in Toyland, a very special place where you can see all sorts of different toys coming and going. Everyone here is ever so nice, except the naughty goblins, of course. They're not very nice to me at all! You'll soon be reading about all my Toyland adventures in this new Noddy Annual, but first let me tell you about some of the toys you are going to meet...

NODDY'S CAR

This is my little red and yellow car. We drive around Toy Town together, taking passengers for sixpence a ride. It's a very clever car, because it talks to me with the 'Parp! Parp!' of its horn!

BIG-EARS

Big-Ears the Brownie is my best friend. I often visit him in his toadstool house in Toadstool Wood and he gives me lots of lovely tea and cakes!

TESSIE BEAR

I love Tessie Bear because she is always kind to everyone. She never gets cross, even when her Bumpy Dog knocks me over - which happens rather a lot!

MR. PLOD

Every town needs a good policeman, and Mr. Plod is ours. He keeps Toy Town in order and often tells me off for driving too fast!

MARTHA MONKEY

One of my regular passengers is Martha, the toy monkey. Her tail is so long that she often has trouble getting into my taxi!

MR JUMBO

Someone else who only just fits into my little car is Mr. Jumbo. He is very jolly, but the car leans to one side when he is in the passenger seat!

DINAH DOLL

There is a very good market in Toy Town and the best stall there is run by my friend, Dinah Doll. If ever I have any sixpences to spend, I buy something from her.

SLY

There are lots of naughty goblins in Toy Town and Sly is one of them. They live nearby in the Dark Wood and come into town to cause mischief. Sly often plays tricks on me and I don't like it one bit!

GOBBO

When Sly is being naughty, he is usually with his friend, Gobbo. They always get caught. One of their favourite tricks is stealing my shopping. That makes me very cross indeed!

NODDY IN TOYLAND

I'm a little nodding boy,
I always nod my head,
Except of course when I'm asleep
And cuddled up in bed.

My hat is blue,
It fits me well
And at the top
There is a bell,
So when I nod
You'll hear it ring,
Tinkle, tinkle,
Jingle, jing.

My little head is on a spring,
So tap it and you'll see
How it goes niddy-niddy-nod,
As happy as can be!

NODDY'S NUMBERS

Noddy loves counting games. Count the things below, then use a pencil to practise writing your numbers with Noddy.

1 1 1 1

2 2 2 2

3 3 3 3

4 4 4 4

TESSIE BEAR'S UMBRELLA

Tessie Bear was walking through Toy Town one afternoon. It began to rain.

She put up her umbrella, but a gust of wind swept her down the high street.

The wind blew her into the Skittle family and she knocked them all over.

She bowled Bert Monkey over, too. Oh, what a very windy day it was!

Tessie Bear bumped into Mr. Wobbly-Man. He wobbled and wobbled!

She knocked Mr. Plod over, too. He was a very cross policeman indeed.

"Tessie Bear, I'm arresting you for breaking the speed limit!" he said sternly.

The umbrella blew him away, too! Don't break the speed limit, Mr. Plod!

DINAH DOLL'S UMBRELLA'S

Dinah Doll sells umbrellas on her stall, so she likes rainy days! Look at the four umbrellas below. They all look the same, but one is different. Which umbrella is the odd one out? Say why it is different to the other three umbrellas. The answer is at the bottom of the page.

1

2

3

4

Answer: Umbrella number 2 is the odd one out because it has stars on it, not dots.

14

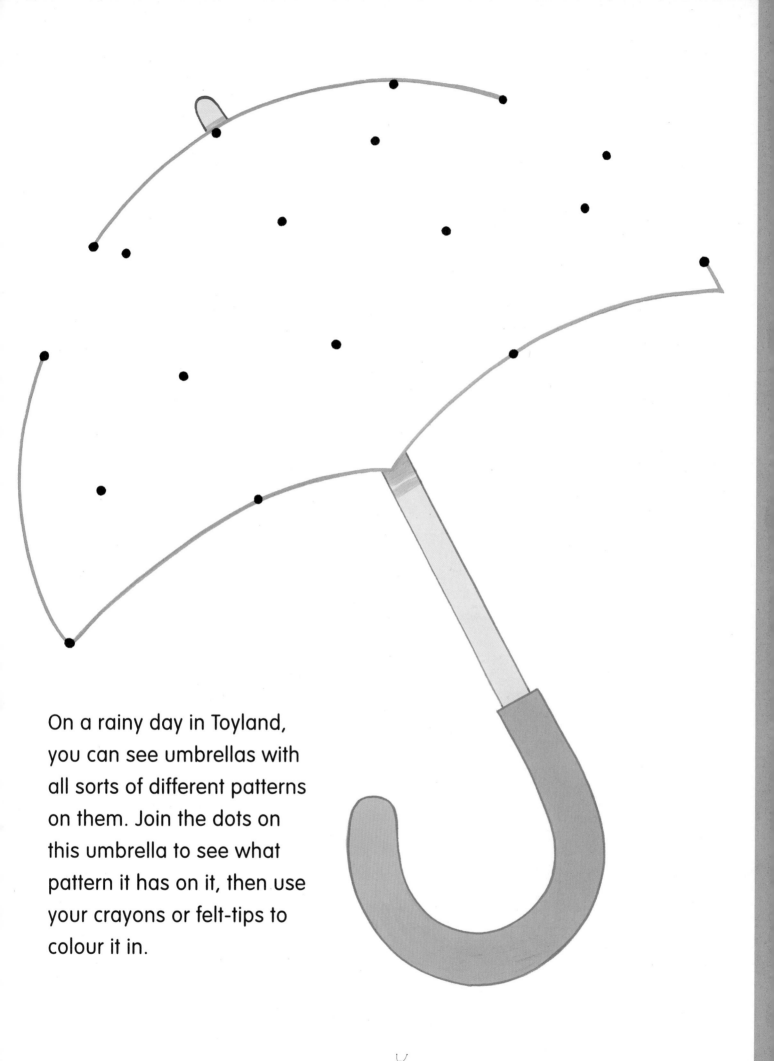

On a rainy day in Toyland, you can see umbrellas with all sorts of different patterns on them. Join the dots on this umbrella to see what pattern it has on it, then use your crayons or felt-tips to colour it in.

PRETTY SNOWFLAKES

Noddy loves playing in the rain, but he thinks that snow is even more fun! Did you know that snowflakes have six points, and that no two snowflakes are the same? Next time it snows, catch some snowflakes on your glove and have a close look at their shape. You need look quickly, as they will soon melt on your warm hand!

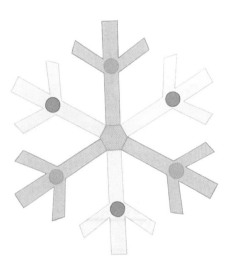

Here is a picture of a pretty snow flake. Use your pencil or crayon to draw some more to go with it.

I LIKE SLEDGING

Even though it's very chilly,
I always go to somewhere hilly
When Toyland is under
lots of snow.
I take my little sledge
And I climb up to the edge,
Then down the hill, like lightning,
I go!

I slide down at such a pace,
It's even better when I race
With Master Tubby, or whoever
wants a try,
Up the hill again we run,
As we say, "Sledging is such fun,
For when we sledge, we feel like
we can fly!"

NODDY AND THE SNOWMAN

One night in Toyland, it snowed and snowed. Early the next morning, Noddy and his friends wrapped up warm and came out to have fun in the snow.

Noddy threw a snowball at Martha Monkey. She was so startled, she slipped over. "That was naughty, Noddy!" she shouted crossly, as he ran away from her. "Why don't you go and snowball the Skittle family? They are meant to fall down!"

Martha was right. Noddy threw snowballs at the skittles and they loved falling over in the snow. Mr. Wobbly Man came to join in the fun and Noddy threw a snowball at him, too. Mr. Wobbly Man didn't fall over. He just wobbled and wobbled.

That afternoon, Noddy and Big-Ears decided to build a snowman in Noddy's garden. "I'll go and find a hat for him," said Noddy when it was finished.

Noddy borrowed a hat and scarf from Tessie Bear and put them on the snowman. "What a fine snowman we've made!" smiled Big-Ears.

Noddy and Big-Ears were proud of their snowman. Tessie Bear came to see if her hat and scarf had been of any use. "My goodness!" she smiled. "You have been busy!" Dinah Doll came to look, too. "That's a super snowman!" she exclaimed.

By the end of the afternoon, Noddy and Big-Ears were beginning to feel quite cold. They went inside and Noddy made a nice supper for them both. He said Big-Ears should stay the night, rather than walk through the snowy woods in the dark.

Noddy and Big-Ears said goodnight and went to bed. Noddy was so tired from all that playing in the snow that he went straight to sleep. In the night, the sound of snow falling off the roof woke him with a start. "What was that bump?" he whispered.

Noddy got out of bed and tiptoed all round his little house. Then he heard another bump. "Goodness!" he exclaimed. "It must be burglars!"

Noddy went to the window and looked out. He saw somebody standing quite still in the garden. "Oh, dear!" he gasped. "There's somebody outside!"

Noddy ran into the room where Big-Ears was sleeping soundly. "Big-Ears!" he cried. "Big-Ears, wake up!" He gave his friend a little shake and tried shouting again. "Big-Ears, do stop snoring! I think there's a burglar outside! Wake up!"

Noddy gave Big-Ears such a shake that he woke with a start. "What?" he gasped, sitting up. "A burglar? We'll soon chase him away!"

Big-Ears hurried out of the bedroom to find a broom, while Noddy fetched a saucepan. "Let's sneak out of the back door," said Big-Ears.

Noddy and Big-Ears tiptoed out of the back door as quietly as little mice. "Where did you see him, Noddy?" whispered Big-Ears. "There, look!" replied Noddy, pointing. "He's still there! Go on, Big-Ears, see him off with the broom!"

Big-Ears took a deep breath, then ran at the stranger with his broom held high. "Take that!" he cried, swinging the broom round and hitting him with it. "And that!" shouted Noddy, using the saucepan. "Leave us alone! Out of our garden! Out!"

Noddy and Big-Ears made so much noise that they woke the neighbours. Tessie Bear came out with a lamp to see what was happening. "Are you all right, Noddy?" she called. "Whatever's going on?" asked Mrs. Skittle over the wall.

One of the young skittles ran to fetch Mr. Plod the policeman. "Mr. Plod! Come and arrest this burglar!" said Noddy, when he saw him. "He was prowling around in my garden!" "Really?" gasped Mr. Plod, shining his torch on someone in a hat.

Mr. Plod began to chuckle. "Noddy!" he exclaimed. "You and Big-Ears have been having a fight with the snowman you built today! He's smashed to pieces!" "Oh! After all that work!" said Noddy, as everyone else laughed. "I'm sorry, Big-Ears!"

A SNOWY RIDE THROUGH TOYLAND

Noddy has been at Big-Ears' house all afternoon. The two friends were so busy chatting that they didn't notice all the snow falling outside! It's time for Noddy to drive home now, but he needs to go very carefully in the snow. Show him how to get home without driving into any snowdrifts, and remember not to slow down near the Dark Wood - there are goblins about!

A SNOWY SURPRISE

Don't go to the Dark Wood
When there has been snow,
The paths are too slippy
And the branches hang low,
For there's snow heaped upon them
And down it may fall,
But the thing to fear most
Is a goblin's snowball!

A CHILLY TRICK

Oh, dear! It's a snowy day and Noddy has stopped at the shops for some cocoa. Look what those naughty goblins have put in his car! He's going to get a surprise when he comes back, isn't he?

Look at the two pictures and see if you can spot the 5 differences between them. The answers are at the bottom of the page. Then use your crayons or felt-tips to colour the picture.

Answers: Left Snowman's scarf has lost its spots – Right Snowman's nose is missing Ladybird has a spot missing – A tree has disappeared in the top right corner– A cloud is missing

BIG-EARS' EASTER EGG

It is Easter time. Big-Ears has decided to buy Noddy a chocolate egg.

He has chosen an egg with a bow on it. Now he is cycling up the hill.

Look out, Big-Ears! The egg has fallen off! Oh, dear, he hasn't noticed.

"That special egg was for Noddy!" Big-Ears says sadly when he gets home.

At Noddy's house, Noddy laughs when Big-Ears tells him what happened.

"On my way home, I saw a lovely big egg rolling down the hill," says Noddy.

"I stopped my car and picked it up. Now you can give me the egg, after all!"

Big-Ears gives Noddy his special egg and smiles, "Happy Easter, Noddy!"

A YUMMY EASTER EGG

Big-Ears bought Noddy a special Easter egg with a bow on it in the story. What would you like your Easter egg to look like? Use your crayons or felt-tips to make this egg look extra special. You could even put a bow on it, if you like!

HOLIDAY

Big-Ears tells me
We're off to the sea,
We'll dig in the sand,
Oh, won't it be grand?
We'll paddle and play,
Oh, hip-hip-hooray!

We'll have an ice lolly,
Oh, won't it be jolly?
I can't wait to reach
That big sandy beach,
We're going away
On a big holiday!

NODDY GOES ON HOLIDAY

Summer had arrived in Toyland, but poor Noddy was in bed with a cold. Big Ears decided to go and visit his friend and took some presents to cheer him up.

Based on original story, Noddy Goes to the Seaside

Big-Ears went to Noddy's bedside and asked him how he was feeling. "Oh, Big-Ears," said Noddy, "my head aches and I keep sneezing. I feel terrible!" "Poor little Noddy," smiled Big-Ears. "What you need is a holiday. You've been run down."

"No one ran me down, Big Ears," frowned Noddy, "I've just got a cold." "Noddy, I mean you've been working too hard!" chuckled Big-Ears. "Would you like to go to the seaside soon? The sea air will do you good." Noddy sat up. "Oh, I'd love to!" he beamed.

When Noddy was feeling a little better, Big-Ears came to pick him up. He wrapped Noddy up warm so he wouldn't get another cold.

"I feel like a parcel!" exclaimed Noddy, as they got into the car. Big-Ears said he would drive to give Noddy a rest. Noddy hoped that he would drive carefully.

Noddy felt funny sitting in the passenger seat of his red and yellow car. He secretly thought that Big-Ears wasn't a very good driver! On their way to the seaside, they seemed to go over every bump in Toyland and almost lost Noddy's bag in a big puddle.

Noddy and Big-Ears reached the seaside at last. They walked along the sand and gazed out to sea. "Look how big the sea is, Big-Ears!" smiled Noddy. "It's even bigger than the duck pond in Toy Town. It looks like it goes on for ever!"

Big-Ears rented a little wooden chalet from a friendly fisherman. It was just big enough for two beds, a table and some chairs.

The two friends were very tired from their journey and all that sea air. They went to bed early and slept soundly until morning.

Noddy and Big-Ears had such a lovely time on the beach the next day. They bought buckets and spades and made an enormous sandcastle.

While Big-Ears went to make lunch, Noddy sat on top of the sandcastle and watched the tide coming in. The sea almost splashed his toes!

The sea swept round the sandcastle, so when Noddy looked round he got quite a shock. "Oh, no!" he gasped. "However will I get back to shore?" He rang the bell on his hat and Big-Ears came running out of the chalet. "Help!" Noddy shouted.

Big-Ears laughed when he saw Noddy. "You don't need any help!" he said. "The water's not deep. You can paddle through it." Noddy did just that.

On one morning of the holiday, though, Noddy and Big-Ears did get into deep water. The tide was high and a big wave knocked them both over.

They managed to wade out of the water, but then Noddy saw that his car had been washed out to sea. "Oh, Big-Ears!" wailed Noddy. "What shall we do? I can't rescue my car, I can't swim! Why didn't I learn? Please do something, Big-Ears!"

"Don't worry, Noddy," said Big-Ears. "I'll swim after your car." He hurried off to change into his swimming costume and waded into the sea.

Big-Ears' swimming was much better than his driving! He soon caught up with the little bobbing car and clambered into the driving seat.

Big-Ears began to drive Noddy's car back to shore. It was just like a little boat! The car was very pleased that it had been rescued and even began to enjoy its swim. "Parp! Parp!" it called to Noddy on the beach. Noddy smiled and waved back.

At last Big-Ears drove the car out of the sea. "Hooray for Big-Ears!" cheered Noddy. "You saved my dear little car!" "It's not just a car!" grinned Big-Ears. "It's a car-boat! Isn't it clever?" "Yes," agreed Noddy, his bell jingling, "and that's given me an idea!"

Noddy was feeling so well from his rest that he decided he wanted to work. He began to run his taxi service again, but with a difference. "This way for the car-boat!" he told the toys on the beach. "Only sixpence a ride!" See how busy Noddy is. All aboard!

SEASIDE COUNTING

Noddy is very excited about being at the seaside. There are so many interesting things to see. Help him to count all the things he has seen so far, writing the numbers in the boxes as you do so.

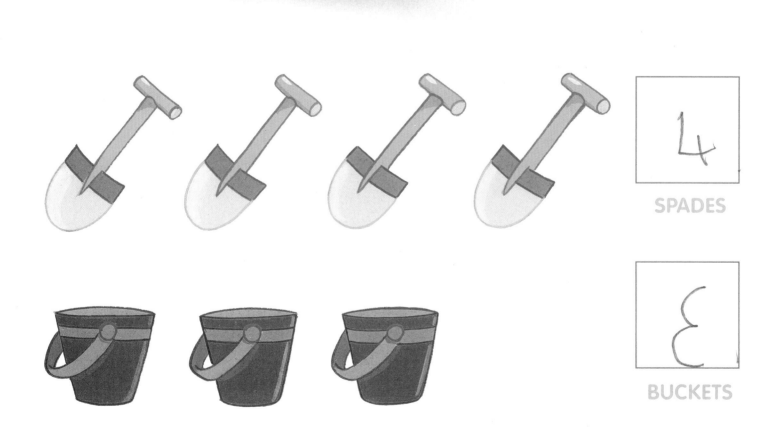

4 SPADES

3 BUCKETS

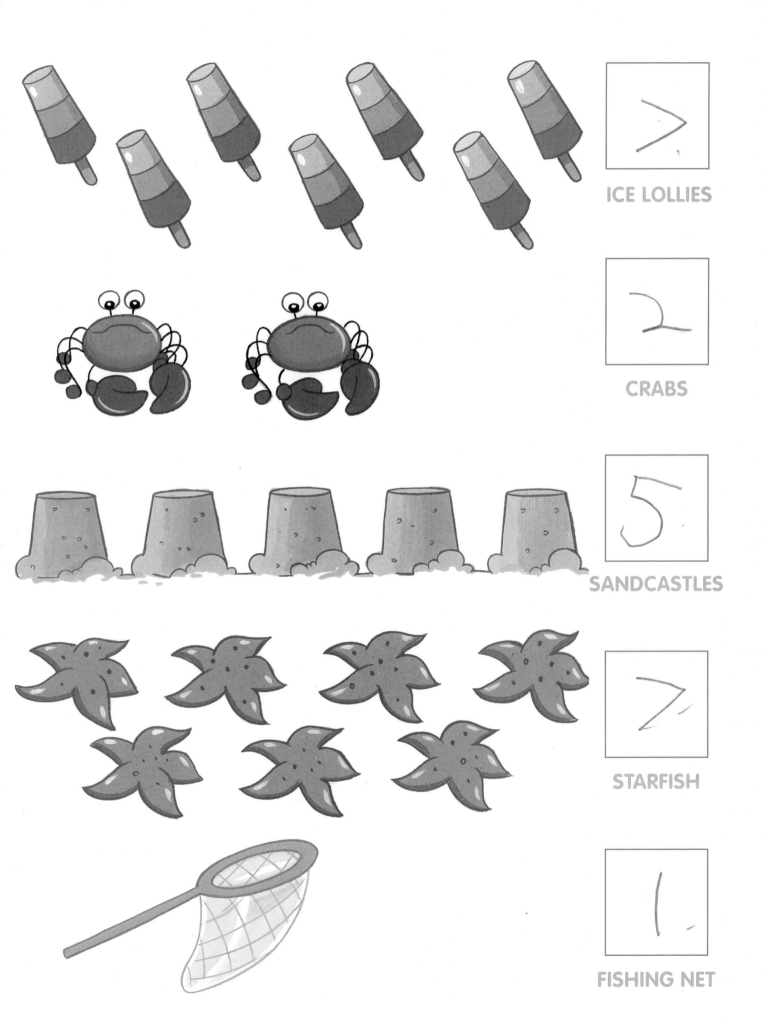

ICE LOLLIES

CRABS

SANDCASTLES

STARFISH

FISHING NET

43

NICE ICES

Noddy thinks the best thing about the seaside is ice-cream!
Fill in the missing letters to find out the flavours of the
ice-creams shown here. The answers are at the
bottom of the page.

st _ a _ ber _ y

l e m o n

ch _ c _ la _ e

v _ ni _ l a

m _ n _

THE SEA

The sea is big,
The sea is blue,
It's big enough
For me and you,
It's big enough
For everybody,
Come and splash
With little Noddy!

THE BIG REWARD

Noddy wanted to borrow some money.
"I don't have any," said Big-Ears.

"Don't look so sad, Noddy!" called
Tessie Bear. "Come shrimping with me."

They had fun shrimping together,
pushing the net round the rock pools.

Did they catch any shrimps? No! Noddy
did catch a pretty necklace, though.

"Take it to the police station," Big-Ears suggested. "There's a reward for it."

Noddy took the necklace to Mr. Plod and collected the reward from him.

"Goodness!" exclaimed Noddy. "There's enough money to buy a big picnic!"

Look at the lovely tea they had on the beach. Well done, little Noddy!

COMING HOME

How nice it is to go away
And have a lovely holiday;
And yet although it's fun to roam,
It's even better coming home,
Coming home,
Coming home,
It's really LOVELY coming home!

BIG-EARS' SOCKS

Big-Ears enjoyed his holiday, but his suitcase
was in a bit of a muddle when he came back!
He thinks he may have left a sock behind, but
he's not sure which one. Help him to pair up
the socks and find out which one is on its own.
The answer is at the bottom of the page.

Answer: Striped orange and yellow sock

49

TIME FOR A STORY

I've had my bath,
I've brushed my teeth,
I've got my 'jamas on,
I'm in my room
with the curtains shut,
Now that the sunshine's gone.

I've climbed in bed,
I'm all tucked up,
I shall not make a peep,
While I hear a bedtime story,
Before I go to sleep...

NODDY'S BEDTIME STORIES

Noddy's Exciting Day
Noddy and the Squeaker

NODDY'S EXCITING DAY

Here comes little Noddy, driving his red and yellow car out of the garage. "Parp! Parp!" goes the hooter, telling everyone that he's coming.

"Does anyone need a taxi ride?" he calls. Toy Town is very busy at this time in the morning. Hello, Mr. Milko. Have you left Noddy a bottle of milk this morning? Here's the postman, too, with a bundle of letters for Noddy.

"Good morning, Noddy!" he calls. "I have some letters for you."

"Put them in my letter-box, please!" Noddy calls back. "I can't stop for them now. Goodbye!"

Noddy drives along, humming a little song: "I'm happy today, hip-hip-hooray!" Ah, here's Martha Monkey and she's waving to Noddy.

"Noddy! Stop, please! I want to go and get a birthday present for my aunty."

Noddy stops the car and opens the door for Martha.

"Hello, Martha," he says. "Where would you like to go?"

"To the sweet shop, please," Martha replies. "My aunty likes chocolates. I think I'll buy her a big box of them."

"You like chocolates, too, don't you, Martha?" says Noddy, driving off.

"Aha! You're buying your aunty chocolates so that she'll give you some. I know what you're up to, Martha!"

Soon they arrive at the sweet shop and Martha jumps out.

"Here it is," she says. "Ooh, what a lovely, big box of chocolates I can

see in the window. I wonder if I have enough money to buy them."

"Well, you must pay me sixpence for your ride first," insists Noddy. Martha pays Noddy and goes into the shop.

"I hope someone else needs a taxi soon," Noddy thinks to himself. "I've only had one passenger this morning."

"Hello, Noddy!" someone calls. Noddy looks and there is Mr. Jumbo. "Could you take me home, please?" he asks. "I've been for a walk and my feet are too tired to take me home."

"Get in, Mr. Jumbo!" Noddy smiles, even though the car leans to one side when heavy Mr. Jumbo is in it.
Off they go. As they drive round the bay, they hear music. "Oh, look, Noddy," says Mr. Jumbo. "It's a funfair! Shall we stop and have a look?"

"Ooh, yes," agrees Noddy. "Look, there's a merry-go-round, Mr. Jumbo. That's where all the music is coming from."

What a lovely fair it is. There's a coconut shy, too, and Clockwork Mouse is trying to win a prize.

There are swings as well. How high they go!

"I want to go on the merry-go-round! I want to go on the swings!" shouts Noddy. "I want to knock down a coconut!"

"Well, as you have driven me here, I shall pay for you," says Mr. Jumbo, and he puts his long trunk into his pocket and pulls out his money.

Noddy loves the fair. First, he goes on the merry-go-round. His horse goes up and down, as well as round and round. Then he and Mr. Jumbo go on the swings that go round and round and fly out into the air as they go. Noddy's hat falls off while he is on the swings, so the merry-go-round man picks it up and gives it back to him when he gets off.

"You need to pin it on!" he says.

Mr. Jumbo and Noddy go on the helter-skelter next. What fun it is! Oh, dear. What's happened to Mr. Jumbo?

He's got stuck! He can't get round that corner.

"Help!" he shouts. "Help, Noddy!"

Then someone bumps into him from behind and he shoots down to the bottom. Goodness, what a bump!

"I shall never go down a helter-skelter again," says Mr. Jumbo. "It's not safe!"

Big-Ears arrives at the fair, looking worried.

"I was riding by on my

bicycle, looking for you, Noddy," he says, "and I saw someone jump into your car and drive it away! It looked like naughty Gobbo, the goblin."

"Oh, no! My dear little car!" cries Noddy.

"Look!" exclaims Big-Ears. "There goes your car on the ferry. I'll get a speed boat and we'll go after it!"

Big-Ears borrows a little speed boat and Noddy climbs in next to him. Then they see Mr. Plod the policeman on the jetty.

"Mr. Plod! We're going after Noddy's car, it's been stolen by a goblin!" shouts Big-Ears. "Jump in!"

There go all three of them after the ferry.

"Rrrr-r-r-r-r-r!" goes the speed boat. It's going very fast and soon catches up with Gobbo. How frightened he is when he sees Mr. Plod coming!

"Stop!" shouts Mr. Plod in his sternest voice. "Stop, I say! How dare you take Noddy's car!"

The ferry boat stops. Mr. Plod and Noddy climb on board. Mr. Plod takes hold of Gobbo so that he can't escape.

"I'll have my car back back now, thank you," says Noddy. "Parp! Parp!" toots the little car as it is lowered into the speed boat. It is very pleased to see Noddy. "Rrrrr-r-r-r-r-r!" Off they go, back over the water to the jetty, where everyone is waiting to cheer them.

"Mr. Plod's taking Gobbo to the police station!" Noddy calls to them.

"And I've got my car back safely, look!"

"Hooray!" they all shout. "Hip-hip-hooray!"

Sammy Sailor helps Noddy to get the car out of the speed boat and it

is soon safely on the jetty. Now Noddy can drive it again.

"Why don't you come back to my house, Noddy?" says Big-Ears. "We need a rest after all that excitement!"

"What a good idea!" agrees Noddy. "I don't think I want to pick up any more passengers today."

He ties Big-Ears' bicycle to the back of his car and they set off for tea at the toadstool house. "I'm ready for a nice piece of cake now, Big-Ears," Noddy smiles to his friend. "It really has been a very exciting day!"

NODDY AND THE SQUEAKER

It was Dinah Doll's birthday and she was having a little party to celebrate. It was a very nice party indeed, with crackers, balloons, cakes, ice-cream and lemonade.

Noddy was very surprised to hear a bang when he pulled a cracker with Big-Ears. He was so startled, he fell right over! He wouldn't even open the rolled up paper hat that had jumped out, in case that went BANG as well.

"It won't make a noise, Noddy," smiled Big-Ears. "Open the hat and put it on. It'll be all right, I promise!"

The hat didn't go bang, of course, so Noddy put it on over his own hat. It looked very funny, because it was a paper crown, but Noddy said he didn't want to take off his own hat in case it got lost.

Noddy pulled another cracker, and this time he didn't mind the bang. He got something peculiar out of it - a little flat, plastic thing that looked rather like a biscuit. When Noddy nibbled it, though, it didn't taste very nice.

"What's this, Big-Ears?" he asked, holding it out to him.

"Put it in your pocket for now, Noddy," said Big-Ears. "We're going to play Pass the Parcel."

Noddy put the squeaker into his pocket, not knowing what it did. It was just a little plastic thing that squeaked when it was pressed, but Noddy

hadn't pressed it, so he didn't know that.

Everyone sat down to play Pass the Parcel. When Noddy sat down, he sat on the squeaker.

"EEEEEEE!" went the squeaker. Noddy was very surprised.

"Oh, dear! I think I've sat on a cat!" he exclaimed, getting up. He looked, but there was no cat there,

of course. Noddy sat back down. "EEEEEEE!" went the squeaker again. Noddy jumped up.

"Goodness gracious!" he said, alarmed. "Who is it, squeaking like that?"

"Do sit down, Noddy," said Dinah Doll. "Every time I try to pass you the parcel, you jump up!"

Noddy sat down again, but this time the game music was so loud that he didn't hear the squeak. He didn't get up again until the game was over and he had quite forgotten about the noise that had puzzled him.

The next game was Musical Bumps. Miss Pink Cat played the piano and everyone danced about. When she suddenly stopped playing, everyone sat down quickly with a BUMP! The last one to sit down was out.

Noddy danced about merrily with all the others. The music stopped and he sat down with a bump.

"EEEEEEEEEE!"

Noddy sprang up and looked round.

"What's the matter?" asked Big-Ears.

"I'm sure I keep sitting on a cat," Noddy replied. "I sit on it and it squeaks."

"You can see there's no cat, Noddy," said Big-Ears, "except Miss Pink Cat, and you didn't sit on her, did you?"

The music began again. Noddy liked dancing, because his bell always tinkled merrily and his head nod-nod-nodded.

The music stopped. Down everyone went with a BUMP!

"Eeeee-EEEEE!"

"That cat again!" cried Noddy. "Where IS it?"

"Noddy, you're out!" called Miss Pink Cat. "Go and sit down until the game's finished."

Noddy flopped into a big armchair, thinking that the cat must be a special, invisible one.

"EEEEEEEEEEE!"

"Oh, you silly cat!" shouted Noddy, getting up to look in the chair. He flung the cushions on the floor, he put his hand down the sides of the chair; he even looked underneath it.

"Here, puss, puss!" he called. "Where are you?"

Everyone looked at him in astonishment.

"Noddy, you are funny," said Big-Ears. "Why do you think there's a cat about?"

"Well, every time I sit down, it miaows," Noddy explained. "Listen."

He sat down in the chair with a bump and, of course, the squeaker squeaked:

"EEEEEEEE!"

Noddy leapt up and Big-Ears began to laugh.

"Oh, Noddy!" he chuckled. "That's not a cat, it's just the squeaker you got from the cracker! You put it in your pocket, so I expect you keep sitting on it."

Noddy dug deep into his pocket and pulled out the squeaker. He squeezed it and it squeaked.

"Oh, yes," he said, "that's what I kept sitting on. What a funny noise it makes! I think it's super, I shall squeak it all day long!"

Noddy did just that. He squeaked it and squeaked it so much that by the end of the afternoon, the squeak had worn out. Big-Ears was really quite glad about that!

TIME FOR BED

My story's told, I've had my kiss
And now it's time for bed,
I think I'll plump my pillow up
Before I rest my head.

I've said goodnight,
I'm all curled up,
I've checked my nightlight's on,
I hope I have exciting dreams
That last the whole
night long!

I'M A HAPPY FELLOW

I'm a happy fellow,
I've a car of red and yellow,
I drive it slow or fast
Until we're there at last!

I'm a happy fellow,
I've a very cheery 'Hello!'
'Parp! Parp!' goes my car,
You can hear it from afar!

NODDY'S FAVORITE THINGS

Noddy enjoyed Dinah Doll's party very much. He especially liked eating all his favourite foods. Look at all the nice things to eat. Are they your favourites, too? Draw over the letters with a pencil and you can write the names of all the tasty treats. What other things do you like to eat?

tarts

cake

 jelly

 crisps

 ice-cream

buns

 rolls

BAKE A CAKE

Mrs. Tubby Bear loves baking and often makes birthday cakes for her friends in Toy Town. She is going to bake a cake now. Which of the things shown here do you think she will need? The answers are at the bottom of the page.

OH! WHAT SHALL I EAT AT THE PARTY?

Oh, what shall I eat at
the party?
Oh, WHAT shall I eat at
the party?
I think I will start
With a little jam tart,
And then I will take
A big slice of cake

And a chocolate bun
(I'll only take one)
And a jelly that shakes
And quivers and quakes,
Some lemonade, too,
And a biscuit or two
And...well, I am sure
I won't eat any more!
That's what I'll eat at the party,
Yes, that's what I'll eat at
the party!

THE SKITTLES PARTY

Noddy took Mrs. Skittle on a shopping trip round Toy Town in his taxi.

Mrs. Skittle bought cakes, juice and balloons. She was doing a tea-party.

Noddy drove her home and helped her in with all her parcels and bags.

The Skittle children were still out playing. Mrs. Skittle picked up her bell.

She gave it to Noddy and asked him to ring it. Oh, dear! The bell was broken!

"I shall never get the children in now," she said. "They won't hear me calling."

Noddy had an idea. He took off his hat and began to shake the bell on it.

The children heard the bell and came in for tea. Have some cake, Noddy!

SOMETHING BEGINNING WITH 'T'

Here comes the Toyland Train! Look carefully at this picture. As well as the Toyland Train, there are seven other things that begin with 't'. Can you can find them all? The answers are at the bottom of the page. How many other words beginning with 't' can you think of?

Answers: Apart from the train, you can see a track, a tunnel, Tessie Bear, a tortoise, a toadstool, a tractor and a tree in the picture.

TOYLAND TRAIN

Oh, isn't it fun when the Toyland Train
Goes huffing and puffing along,
And all the trucks on their
wooden wheels
Are singing a rattly song?
We're slowing down for Teddy Bear Town
And now we're off again.

Far away at the end of the day
There's a land of Once Upon a Time,
Far away where the bluebirds play
All the world's a nursery rhyme,
So we'll go all the way
To the end of the day
Till we reach our homes again,
Singing choo-choo-chuffitty-chuffitty
All aboard the Toyland Train!

NODDY GOES FISHING

It was a fine summer's day in Toyland. "It's a perfect day for fishing," Noddy thought to himself. He drove his car through the countryside until he found a pretty little lake and began to fish in it.

Noddy soon reeled in his first catch. What a strange thing - he pulled out a little table! "That'll make a good present for Big-Ears!" he exclaimed. He fished a little more and got another bite. "Goodness!" he chuckled, as he saw his catch. "A chair!"

"I could give that chair to Tessie Bear," Noddy thought, as he threw his line in again. This time he fished out a little bed. It even had sheets and blankets on it. "What a funny thing!" said Noddy. "I wonder who has thrown all this furniture away!"

Noddy decided that Miss Pink Cat would like the bed he'd found. He spent the whole morning fishing in the lake and by lunchtime, he'd fished up enough furniture to fill a little house. It took him the rest of the day to take the presents to all his friends.

Everyone was very pleased with their things, especially Miss Pink Cat. "What a dear little bed!" she exclaimed, giving Noddy a hug. "Thank you!"

The next day, there was a knock at Noddy's door. There stood a very angry water pixie. "You've taken all my furniture and I'd like it back!" she frowned.

"B-b-but I didn't know it was yours!" stammered Noddy. "I've given it all away!" "Given it away?" gasped the pixie. She burst into floods of tears.

Noddy wasn't sure what to do. He put his arm round the pixie and sat her down. "I know!" he said after thinking for a moment. "I'll build you a house!"

Noddy rushed off to buy a box of bricks and the pixie helped him to put them together by the lake. While they were building, she told him that her name was Miss Bubble and that she had always wanted to live in a proper house, on land.

Oh, dear! Do you see what Noddy did? He bought the wrong building blocks! "I may be fed up of living in the water, Noddy," said Miss Bubble, "but I don't think I'd like to live in a railway station!" Noddy took down the bricks and went to change them.

Poor Noddy! He still didn't have the right bricks. "It's very nice, Noddy," said the water pixie, "but I don't really want to live in a shop, either!"

Noddy told Big-Ears what had happened. "Come on, Noddy," he chuckled, "I'll help you to pack away these bricks and get the right ones."

Big-Ears and Noddy set to work with the new bricks and before long they had made a pretty little cottage. "Here's the chimney," said Noddy. "Could you help me with it, Big-Ears?" Some of the other toys came to see what they were doing.

Of course, Miss Bubble's new house needed some furniture. Noddy's friends were only too happy to bring back the things he'd given them. Big-Ears went to get the little table, Tessie Bear brought back the chair and Miss Pink Cat gave back the bed.

As well as getting her furniture back, Miss Bubble was given lots of new presents by the people in Toy Town. "Thank you, everyone," she smiled.

"Oh, Noddy, I'm so pleased with my new house and my new friends," said the little pixie, dancing with happiness. "Let's have a tea-party to celebrate."

Well, everyone loves a tea-party. The whole of Toy Town came, bringing lots of nice things to eat and drink. "I shall call my lovely new house Splash Cottage," announced Miss Bubble, cutting the big cake that Mrs. Tubby had brought.

Miss Bubble decided that she would decorate the outside of her new house with lots of different kinds of shell. Mr. Sparks even painted a sign for it. The little pixie was delighted to have a real house of her own. Doesn't it look pretty?

In fact, Splash Cottage was so pretty that it became famous all over Toyland. Everyone wanted to see it, so Noddy was busy for quite a time, taking people to and fro in his taxi. It was lucky for both Miss Bubble and Noddy that he went fishing that day!

MISS BUBBLE'S MUDDLE

Miss Bubble is sorting out her furniture that Noddy fished out of the lake. See if you can help her by drawing lines between the things that go together. The answers are at the bottom of the page.

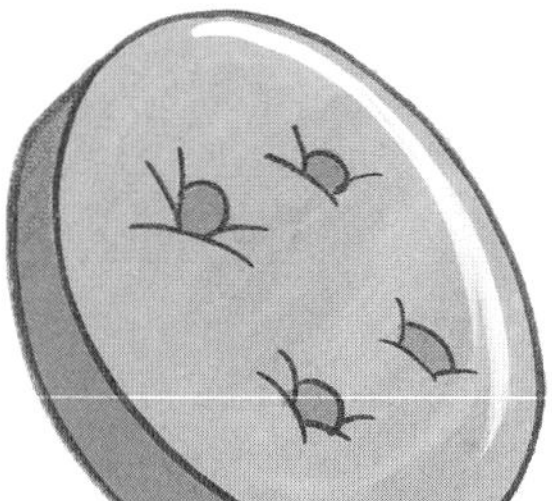

1

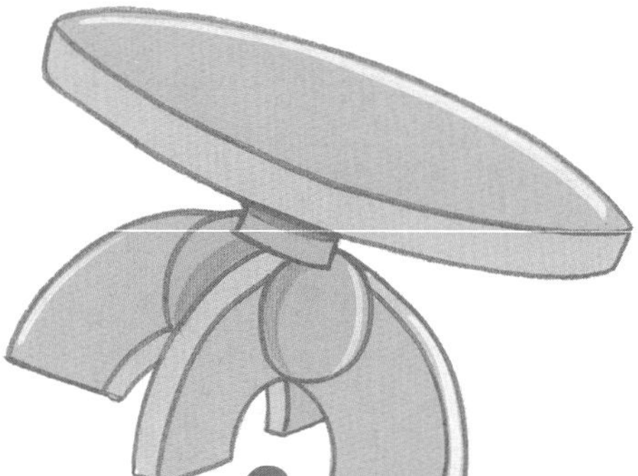

2

3

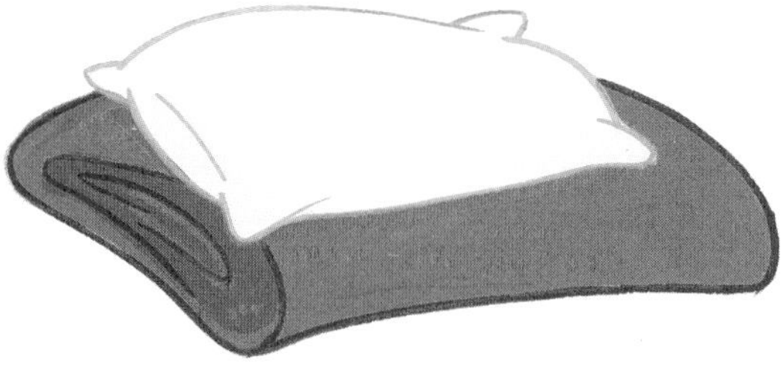

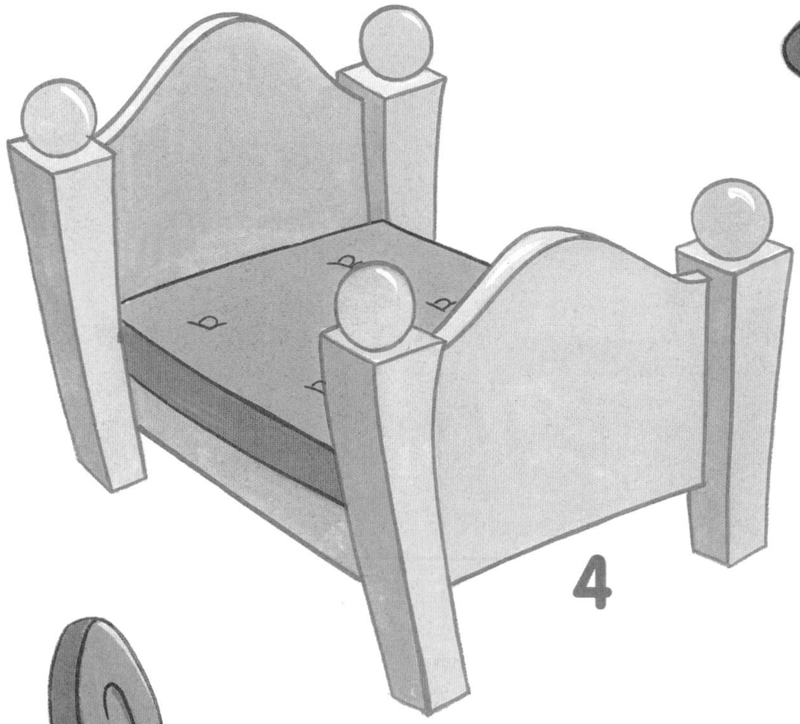

4

5

6

LITTLE MISS BUBBLE

Little Miss Bubble
Had a little bit of trouble
When somebody took all
her things.

First her table, then her chair
Floated right up there,
Until all she had left were
her wings!

She said, "For goodness' sake!"
And she swam from her lake
To find the thief was a little boy
called Noddy.

But she did not have to worry,
For Noddy said, "I'm very sorry!"
And he built a cottage, pretty
as can be.

WHERE IS NODDY'S SHOPPING?

Noddy has stopped in the Dark Wood on his way to Big-Ears' house. What is Sly doing? He is talking to him while the other goblins steal poor Noddy's shopping and hide it. What a naughty trick! Luckily, Big-Ears has come to meet Noddy and can see what is happening. Those goblins are in for a stern telling off!
Help Big-Ears to find all eight of Noddy's parcels, then use your crayons or pens to colour the picture.

THE ROLLER-BLADE RIDE

One day, the Toy Town toy shop had some roller-blades in the window.

All the toys were very excited about them. Almost everyone bought a pair.

The goblins couldn't wait to put theirs on. Even Mr. Jumbo had a pair!

Gobbo tied himself to the back of Noddy's car and waited for Noddy.

Noddy didn't see naughty Gobbo and drove away. What fun Gobbo had!

He took Martha Monkey's hand and she took Clockwork Mouse's hand.

There was soon a long line of toys roller-blading behind Noddy's car. Mr. Jumbo joined in and Noddy's little car had to stop. Noddy was cross!

NODDY'S ROLLER-BLADE RIDE

Join in the story by saying what the pictures are as they appear.

 saw the other toys with their  and

decided to join in the fun. He stopped his

outside the toy shop and went in to buy a pair.

 put on his  and went to show

"Watch this!" shouted , and he sped down a hill

on his new . "BE CAREFUL!" called .

"I'm all right!" laughed . Bump! bumped

into a . "Oh, dear," he said. "Perhaps I should

have listened to  after all!"

TOYLAND

Come to Toyland and you'll meet
Clockwork clowns on every street,
Little dolls with curly hair
And a big, fat teddy bear.

Wobbly men you're sure to see,
And skittles going home to tea,
Coloured balls that bounce up high
And wooden soldiers marching by.

All the animals from the ark,
Funny dogs that bark and bark,
Naughty goblins, a rocking horse
And Noddy in his car, of course!

TOYLAND FAVOURITES

On this page are some of the things that you might spot if you have a walk round Toy Town. Look at each one and say which of the characters on the opposite page would be seen with it. The answers are at the bottom of the opposite page.

Answer: The basket is Tessie Bear's, the crate is Mr. Milko's, the fishing rod belongs to Sammy Sailor, the petrol pump is in Mr. Sparks' garage and the bicycle is Big-Ears'.

MR STRAW'S EMERGENCY

One sunny afternoon, Noddy was taking Mr. Noah back to the ark in his taxi. Mr. Noah had been to visit some friends in Toy Town and was going back to feed his animals.

*Based on original story,
Noddy is a Great Help*

Noddy was rather enjoying the drive through the countryside, when Mr. Noah let out a sudden cry. "Look, Noddy! What's that?" Noddy looked to where Mr. Noah was pointing. "It looks like smoke!" exclaimed Noddy. "It's coming from Mr. Straw's farm!"

Noddy drove up to the farm and towards the smoke. It was coming from a haystack that was on fire. Mr. Straw was throwing buckets of water on it to try and put the fire out. "Do you need some help?" shouted Noddy, running through the gate.

"Noddy! It's no good!" cried Mr. Straw. "These buckets of water aren't putting the fire out. I think we need to call the fire brigade!"

Mr. Noah ran as fast as he could to the farmhouse and dialled the emergency number. "There's a fire at Mr. Straw's farm!" he exclaimed.

Mr. Straw and Noddy carried on throwing water at the blazing haystack. "Let's hope we can stop it spreading!" said Mr. Straw. It wasn't long before the duck pond was almost empty. The ducks weren't a bit happy and quacked crossly: "Quack! Quack!"

"Oh, where has that fire engine got to?" wailed Mr. Straw. "There's no pond water left now. If they don't hurry, this fire will reach the farmhouse!"

"Don't worry, Mr. Straw," said Noddy. "I'll go and see what's happened." Noddy jumped in his car and drove out of the farm. "Parp! Parp!" tooted the car.

Noddy sped back along the road to Toy Town and soon came across the fire engine. "The fire engine's broken down, Noddy!" the fireman explained to him. "It just won't move!" Noddy thought for a moment, then his little bell began to jingle.

Noddy's little bell jingled whenever he had a good idea. "I know what we should do!" he exclaimed. "My car can pull you along!" "Parp!" agreed the car.

Noddy fetched a piece of rope from his car boot and tied one end to his back bumper. Then he tied the other end to the fire engine's front bumper.

Noddy's car was smaller than the fire engine, so it had a difficult job to do. "Pull, little car, pull!" called Noddy. The car pulled and pulled, until at last it began to move, taking the fire engine with it. "Hurray!" cheered Noddy, as they set off.

The car and the fire engine soon arrived at Mr. Straw's farm. "We're here, Mr. Straw!" shouted Noddy from the gate. "The fire will soon be out, don't worry!" The fireman jumped out of his fire engine, unravelled the hose and switched it on.

The fireman poured water on the blazing haystack until the fire died down. Mr. Straw smiled with relief. "Thank you, Noddy," he said. "You saved my farm!" "Thank my car, not me!" said Noddy. Can you guess what the car said? "Parp! Parp!"

FIRE!

The firefighters jump when the fire bell rings,
They run round the station and grab all their things:
Big, yellow helmets and heavy, black boots,
Hung on the pegs are their fireproof suits,

The fire engine's waiting, gleaming and bright,
With its shiny, red paint and its blue flashing light,

Through Toyland it speeds with its loud siren on
Till it stops at the fire and out the firefighters run.

They grab the long hoses to point at the blaze,
"All hoses on!" the chief firefighter says,
The flames soon get smaller, the fire dies down
And the firefighters are heroes all over Toy Town!

WHOSE HOSE?

Noddy, Mr. Straw and a Toy Town firefighter each have a hose to put out the fire on the farm. Only one of them is hitting their target, though! Can you see who is spraying water at the haystack? The answer is at the bottom of the page.

Answers: The firefighter's hose is spraying water at the haystack.

HELLO, GOBBO GOBLIN

This is Gobbo, the naughty goblin. He lives in the Dark Wood with the other goblins and is always up to mischief with his friend, Sly.

Use your crayons or felt-tip pens to colour in this picture of Gobbo Goblin. See if you can match the colours to those on the opposite page.

BUMPITY DOG!

Bumpy Dog cannot stay still for a moment! Look at the shadows below and say which one exactly matches the picture. The answer is at the bottom of the page.

1

2

3

4

Answer: Shadow number 3 matches the picture.

Bumpy Dog has been busy in the garden, digging up bones. Look carefully at the pile he has made and say how many bones he has dug up. The answer is at the bottom of the page.

Answer: Bumpy Dog has a pile of 10 bones.

CLEVER BUMPY DOG

Noddy went shopping with Bumpy Dog. He put his bags in the car.

While they had an ice-cream, Clockwork Clown decided to take the bags.

He ran away with the shopping. "After him, Bumpy!" shouted Noddy.

Bumpy Dog scampered after the naughty clown and jumped up at him.

Bumpy took the clown's key and gave it to Noddy. Clockwork Clown ran on.

Noddy and Bumpy jumped into the car to chase after Clockwork Clown.

The clown slowed down to a stop. Noddy soon caught up with him . . .

. . . and so did Mr. Plod. Now Clockwork Clown really is in a lot of bother!

A CHASE THROUGH TOY TOWN

Those naughty goblins have been stealing shopping again! Someone needs to catch them and take them to Toy Town police station for a telling off. To chase Sly and Gobbo through Toy Town, you need a counter for each player and a dice. Each player decides if they are going to be Noddy, Big-Ears, Sammy Sailor or Mr. Plod.

Dinah Doll is having a sale! Miss a go to buy something.

Borrow some roller-blades and speed on two squares.

BUMP! You
Mr. Wobbly
turn to s

Bert Monkey
sends you the
wrong way. Go back
two squares.

Take turns to throw the
dice and run round the
board - you must get a
six to start your chase.
The first to reach the
Dark Wood and catch
the cheeky goblins is
the winner!

Clockwork
Mouse
shows you a short cut.
Run on two squares.

nto
iss a